Murder at The Tavern
A Guilford Mystery

MURDER AT THE TAVERN

A GUILFORD MYSTERY

Juliana Harris

Murder at The Tavern: A Guilford Mystery
©2020, Juliana Harris

Cover Painting: *The Medad Stone Tavern*, pastel by Karen Wiesner, Madison, CT.

Book Design by Jennifer Payne (Words by Jen, Branford, CT)

ISBN: 978-0-578-66318-0

Printed in the U.S.A.

ACKNOWLEDGMENTS

To The Guilford Poets Guild
for listening, and to Bruce Denison
for invaluable advice on
police procedural.

IN MEMORY OF RUFUS BISHOP

CHAPTER **ONE**

CHERYL HENDERSON was late for the PTO meeting. "Of course I'm late," she thought, as she hurried across the dimly lit parking lot, "with Fred out of town and the girls picking at their dinner, why wouldn't I be late?" She was so busy focusing on the entrance to the school she didn't notice a figure coming up the hill to her right until he spoke to her.

"Good evening, Cheryl," said the tall shadow beside her.

"Oh, Squire, I didn't see you. You startled me!"

"Yes, it is dark out this evening, isn't it? How are Fred and your daughters?" this said with a slight bow of the older gentleman's bony shoulders which were covered, as was his custom, in a well-worn woolen cape.

"Everybody's fine, thank you for asking." *What's he doing out here at this time of night?*

"Please give them all my best. A pleasure to see you, as always."

And with another bow and a tip of his wide brimmed hat, Ashley Hamilton Reynolds disappeared into the night.

She would remember this encounter when the article appeared on the front page of the *Guilford Courier* the following week. "Waitress' Body Found in Woods Behind Medad Stone Tavern." The woods were located at the end of the Cox School soccer fields. Something nagged at her. "Those woods are over to the left of the school building, aren't they? I can't remember which direction Squire was coming from that night."

"Squire? A murderer? Oh, come on now," Fred chuckled as he stoked the fire in the family room. "Whatever put that idea in your head?" He plopped down on the sofa and picked up the remote. They were having a long-delayed date night since both of their daughters were out of the house on sleepovers.

"I don't know. It just seemed odd to me he would be in that particular place at that time of night, that's all. I know he's always so gracious and courtly, it's hard to think of him doing something like that."

"Well, for one thing, he was probably coming from his brother's house on Dunk Rock, which is on the east side of the school, and from what Jake Donaldson was saying at the barber shop, it was a pretty grisly crime. The girl was a waitress at the coffee shop and she was pretty badly roughed up. I doubt if Squire would have the strength for such a thing. Or if he even knew her."

"Where does he live? I always see him around town and I know he's a member of the Reynolds family. Does he live alone or with family?"

"I have no idea. Even though I've lived here all my life, I've never known much about him. I do know he once had a wife and a daughter and they lived in that house on Dunk Rock, the blue one next to Josh Reynold's big house."

"Was Josh his brother?"

"I think so. I get a little mixed up when it comes to the Reynolds clan. There are so many of them!"

"You said he had a wife and a daughter. What happened to them?"

"If I remember right, there was a bad accident. Squire was driving and fell asleep at the wheel. His wife and their daughter were killed and he had a major nervous breakdown. He had to be institutionalized and was never the same after that."

"Did he work at the foundry?"

"He was a foreman until the accident. After that, the family took care of him. I think he might live in that rooming house on Whitfield Street, which might have been where he was heading the night you ran into him. I think he spends a lot of time at the library."

"Yes, that's where I'm used to seeing him. He always asks after you."

"Well, I knew him when I was a kid. Dad kept his boat at the marina in those days and that was one of Squire's haunts. He came out sailing with us a couple of times, always wearing that cloak and the hat. And, of course, his walking stick. What a character!"

"That's funny. Come to think of it, he didn't have his walking stick with him that night. I don't think I ever saw him without it and you would think he would have it with him for a walk after dark."

"Look, do you want to watch a movie tonight or not? We're running out of time here."

---

*Sorry about the walking stick, old timer.
But I couldn't let them pin it on me, I've
got too much to lose and you've never been
right since you lost your wife and kid.
It's better this way for everybody.*

CHAPTER **TWO**

GRACE REYNOLDS was finishing the morning dishes when she heard a rap on her back door. "Come in, Ash, the door's open."

"Good morning, Grace, how are you today?"

"I'm okay, thanks. This wet weather isn't so good for my sciatica, but, other than that, I'm doing pretty well for an old bat!"

"Nonsense, there's nothing old about you. I'm sorry to trouble you so early in the day but I was wondering if I might have left my walking stick in your umbrella stand."

"Why, is it missing?"

Squire gave his sister-in-law a rueful smile.

"You know I haven't seen it for a week now and I've searched high and low. I just thought I might have forgotten it here."

"Maybe you left it at the library."

"No, I checked there. I thought I might have left it in my writing room but no luck."

Grace knew that the major part of her brother-in-law's life these days was his poetry. He wrote charming descriptions of his home town and she had urged him to get them published. But Squire, in his usual modest way, merely chuckled and patted her hand.

"Speaking of your writing, I was at a meeting of the Ladies Auxiliary last night and they're looking for a fundraiser. I think your poems would be a great way to make some money for the church. I really wish you would think about putting them into book form."

"Oh, Grace, I really don't think my scribblings would be a best seller but that's a very kind idea."

"Kindness has nothing to do with it. Your poems are delightful and a credit to your home town. I want you to think about this. Why don't you check with Charlie Mayfield at Royal Printing about how much it would cost to print up 100 copies and I'll present it at the next Auxiliary meeting."

The bell ringing over the door to Royal Printing interrupted Charlie's phone conversation.

"Somebody just came in Ralph, gotta go. Keep me posted, okay?" He hung up and hurried out to the front desk. "Oh, Squire, nice to see ya."

"Good to see you, Charlie, as always. I'm afraid I'm here on rather a fool's errand, but Grace insisted I talk with you. You see, she wants me to get an estimate from you as to how much it would cost to print up a booklet of some of my poems. She thinks selling the book might be a good way to raise funds for Christ Church."

"Well, I think that sounds like a swell idea, Squire. How many poems are we talking about here?"

"I suppose perhaps 20 or so? Is that enough to make it worth your while?"

"Are we talking about just copy? Or were you thinking of some illustrations?"

"The poems are mainly about Guilford and its inhabitants and history, so I suppose we could include some photographs or drawings of some sort."

"Why don't you let me think about this and get back to you with a rough estimate. Will you be paying for this, or will the church take responsibility?"

"I'll have to discuss that with Grace. She mentioned the Ladies Auxiliary as the beneficiary, maybe they would assume the expense? Why don't we wait and see just what we're dealing with and then we'll determine who will bear the cost?"

"Okay by me. Say, have you heard about this murder case here in town?"

"Murder case? Good lord, no. I guess I've been so busy looking for my walking stick I have been out of the loop. What's going on?"

"Angie Loomis, you know, the waitress at the coffee shop? She was found beaten to death in the woods behind the Medad Stone Tavern last week."

"Dear lord, how dreadful! I'm afraid I don't know anyone by the name of Angie."

"Sure you do, the pretty blond? I seem to remember you two were quite friendly."

"Oh no...you can't mean Angelina."

He went dead white, I thought he was going to pass out!" Charlie was regaling Ralph Ingersoll with the details of his conversation with Squire. Charlie and Ralph were both volunteer deputies on the Guilford police force and totally engrossed in the most exciting event to occur in the town in many moons.

"Called her Angelina, did he? I remember they were pretty chummy. Poor old guy, he probably had a big crush on Angie. I hope he made it worth her while in tips."

"Any further news on the murder weapon?"

"Last I heard they were trolling Sunset Creek. They think she was beaten to death with some kind of a club."

"That's just awful. Who would do such a thing? Think it was a crime of passion? Some kid who wouldn't take no for an answer? Have they done the autopsy?"

"Oh, yeah. That should be interesting. Hold on a sec, somebody on the other line..."

"...Ralph? That was Nat Simpson. He was part of the search party at the creek. They found what they think is the murder weapon and, you're not gonna believe this, it looks like Squire Reynolds' walking stick!"

You called her Angelina but she was
no angel. When she told me she was
knocked up I thought no way, I always
was careful, but then I remembered the time
she came up behind me and put her hands
down the front of my pants. She pushed me
into the men's room and I had her up
against the wall, fast, hard and hot.
I came like a freight train. Uh, oh.

CHAPTER **THREE**

THE HEADLINE in the *Shoreline Times* read: "Selectman Wins Third Term In A Landslide."

Carl Reynolds sat at his desk on the third floor of Town Hall and read it with relish. Looking around his office, he decided it could use some refurbishing. "I'll get Betsy up here to take a look. She's always been good at that sort of thing."

He looked across the room at the bookcase which held a collection of family photographs: Him with Betsy and the boys at Disney World, his father shortly before he died, and his mother looking rather stiff in a studio portrait. There was no picture of his sister, Marybeth, as the two of them were not congenial. "I think Mib never forgave me for being the good looking one," he once said to his wife.

It was true that Mib was never a beauty but she had used her quick wit and her imaginative flair to make a career once she earned her degree from the Prince School of Retailing at Simmons College in Boston. She worked her way up at Filene's, literally starting in the Basement and ending up as the buyer in the couture department. When their father died, leaving her a small bequest, she returned to Guilford and set up shop at the corner of the Green. Within five years MIB...For The Discriminating Woman had turned enough of a profit to pay off the initial investment from the Guilford Savings Bank.

Carl had been helpful in arranging the loan. After graduating from Guilford High with a football scholarship to UConn, he went on to earn a law degree at Quinnipiac and set up shop in offices above the bank. With his charm and good looks he soon established a thriving trade in probate and real estate matters. It didn't hurt that he married Betsy Parsons, his high school sweetheart, once he returned from a tour of duty with the National Guard in Operation Desert Storm. Her father, Norm Parsons, had a very successful law practice which he was more than happy to turn over to his son-in-law and his guidance had been invaluable.

Carl got involved with local politics early in his legal career, serving on various town commissions and attending the monthly Rotary meetings at The Guilford Mooring. When the Republican Town Committee approached him to run for First Selectman, he was delighted. And now this, "a landslide third term!"

The ringing of his cell phone interrupted his reverie. "Hi, Mom. What's up?"

"Hi, dear. You're not going to believe it, but Jake Donaldson has taken Ash in for questioning,"

"Questioning about what?"

"You know about the girl who was murdered in the woods? They think she was beaten to death with your uncle's walking stick!"

CHAPTER **FOUR**

"WHAT IS YOUR FULL NAME, Mr. Reynolds?"

"Ashley Hamilton Reynolds. I was named Ashley because my mother attended *Gone With the Wind* the night she went into labor. She adored Leslie Howard. It's a good thing she didn't name me Rhett!"

"I'm sorry, sir. I'm afraid that was a little before my time." Jake stepped to the door of his office.

"Stacy, would you mind taking Mr. Reynolds fingerprints for me?" Before the young officer could respond, Carl Reynolds came barreling through the door of the station, loaded for bear.

"Hold your horses, Jake. Let's all sit down and have a talk before we go any further."

"Are you representing Mr. Reynolds in this case, Carl?"

"For the time being, until I get a clearer picture of exactly what's going on here."

"Are you and Mr. Reynolds related?"

"Squire is my uncle. Just because he and my father were brothers doesn't prevent me from representing him."

"Okay, let's have a seat in my office and talk this over. Right this way."

Jake's deputy, Chuck Hopwood, had witnessed this scene with some amusement. Jake caught the smirk on his face and said, "Why don't you take your dinner break Chuck? I can handle this."

Once the deputy had left, the threesome sat in his office while Jake produced a photograph from a file on his desk. "This is a picture of the wooden stick that washed up on the side of Sunset Creek this morning. Several people in the search party identified it as belonging to Mr. Reynolds. Is this your walking stick, sir?"

"Don't answer that, Uncle Ash. Do you mean to tell me you dragged my uncle in here on hearsay from some local yahoos?"

"My walking stick! Thank goodness you found it. I've been searching for it all over town!"

"You mean you lost it, sir?"

"It's been missing for over a week. I had no idea what had become of it."

"But you can positively identify it from this photograph?"

"It has my initials carved in the top of it...A.H.R. I whittled it myself from an elm we had to take down on Josh's property."

CHAPTER **FIVE**

THE COFFEE SHOP was bustling even more than usual on this Thursday morning. Charlie and Ralph sat at their usual table, grilling Chuck Hopwood on the latest developments in the "Crime of the Century."

"C'mon guys, you know I can't tell you all the details. I could lose my job! I will tell you that it's definitely Squire's stick. The old dude identified it himself."

Marybeth Reynolds was standing at the counter, waiting for a takeout of black coffee and a corn muffin, when she overheard Chuck's words. She wanted to go over and push his face in but since she was on her way to police headquarters to visit her uncle, she took a deep breath, grabbed her order and headed for the door.

Jake Donaldson was standing behind the front desk when Mib walked in. *Now that's a fine looking woman. She didn't look like that when we were in school but time has been good to her, yes indeed.*

He was unaware that Mib had a crush on him all the way through Guilford High. He was busy being the star center of the basketball team and dating Darlene Proctor, the perky little cheerleader he married after two years at Gateway Community College. Once he had joined the force and was assigned to night duty his first year, Darlene developed a fondness for Southern Comfort and late nights at Dalton's up on Route 80 where she met a salesman with whom she shared a room at the "no-tell-motel" on one too many nights. Following the divorce, Jake went back to school and got a degree in Criminal Justice which led to his being named Chief two years earlier.

"Hey Mib, good to see you. Everything okay at the shop?"

"All is well, thanks. I've brought some coffee and a muffin for my uncle. May I see him?"

"Sure. Come through that door on the right and I'll take you to him." He met her on the other side of the door and led the way to Squire's cell. *His uniform certainly fits him well. He hasn't lost those slim hips and those broad shoulders.*

There were two cells at the end of the corridor and Squire sat stiffly at the edge of the cot in the cell on the left. He broke into a big grin when he saw his niece. "Marybeth, my dear girl, how good to see you!"

"Hi Uncle Ash, sorry I couldn't get here sooner but things have been frantic at the shop. I brought you a little something from the coffee shop. Jake is there a place we could talk? Or do I have to stay with him in his cell."

"No, no. Why don't you step into the conference room. It's just across the hall. I'll bring Squire right in."

The sight of her elegant uncle in these dismal surroundings broke Mib's heart but she hid her pain behind a warm smile when Jake escorted him into the small room a few minutes later.

"I'll leave you two alone to get caught up. I have to warn you that I may have to interrupt if I get word from the Crime Lab." The walking stick was being examined for DNA and, if the results were incriminating, Jake would have to bring Squire to court in New Haven for arraignment.

"Duly warned, thank you, Chief, you've been very kind." Squire turned and gave Jake a firm handshake and, with that, he left them, closing the door behind him.

"Please have a seat, my dear. Thank you for being so thoughtful and bringing me coffee. Your dear mother was here earlier this morning bringing me some fresh clothing and one of her delicious coffee cakes, which the Chief and his staff and I thoroughly enjoyed. I'm afraid the coffee here leaves much to be desired, so a fresh cup from my favorite restaurant is a real treat."

"I'm glad. And, speaking of the coffee shop, did you know the girl who was murdered?"

"Angelina? Yes, yes, I knew her. She was a sweet child and made a point of taking care of me when I would come in for my poached egg. We liked to talk about poetry. She wrote some poems she was kind enough to share with me."

"What kind of poems? Were they any good?"

"Well, I'm really not in any position to judge other people's work. They were love poems, of course. What you would expect from a pretty young girl. However, I gather the object of her devotion was not, as we might say, available?"

"A married man perhaps?"

"Could be, could be. She was very discreet about his identity and I, of course, didn't want to pry."

Their conversation was interrupted by a light tapping on the door. "Sorry, folks, I'm going to have to cut this short. It seems the state crime lab has found traces of Angie's DNA on the walking stick."

The silly bitch wanted to have the
baby. Wanted me to marry her, can you
believe it? I offered to pay for an operation
but she wouldn't budge and that's when
I knew she had to go.

CHAPTER **SIX**

WHEN MIB SIGNED THE LEASE on the small two-story Victorian at the end of the Green she was delighted to find there was a second-floor apartment included. She set up her shop on the first floor and then turned her attention to creating a comfortable living space above.

After her uncle had been taken into custody, Jake had been very helpful in answering any questions but she was aware he couldn't spend all day with her, so she invited him to dinner at her apartment. She opened her door at 7:00 to find him holding a bouquet of daisies and a bottle of wine.

"Oh, Jake, how nice! Please come in."

She took his coat and ushered him into her living room, giving him a chance to make himself at home while she went to the kitchen to get a vase for the flowers.

"Would you like a glass of wine? Or something else?"

"A beer would be good if you have it."

"Heineken okay?"

"Great, thanks."

Jake took an admiring look around the room. The bay window, which Mib had left curtain-less, had a sweeping view of the Green which was dressed in winter white on this frigid night. A small marble fireplace had a crackling fire in its grate and Jake took a seat in the comfortable armchair that flanked a small sofa and a glass topped coffee table.

"You've got a nice place here" he said as Mib placed a glass of beer and a plate of cheese and crackers in front of him.

"Thank you, sir, I had help from my mom on this project. She had a lot of stuff in her attic she was happy to be rid of."

"Well, you did a great job of pulling things together. I'm afraid my apartment is quite spartan compared to this cozy nest. I guess it's a guy thing, although Darlene wasn't much in the domestic area either."

Mib passed him the cheese and crackers and decided to change the subject. She was sure the topic of his marriage was painful to him and she had never liked Darlene anyway.

"Have you heard anything about Squire?"

"Not much, other than he's a model prisoner, as we knew he would be. I guess your mother has been visiting him and I'm sure that's a help to him."

"Has he been assigned an attorney? I know Carl wanted him to hire some high-powered criminal lawyer but Squire just doesn't have the money and he refused to take any from Carl."

"I assume someone from the New Haven public defender's office will take over the case. I know they took a statement from Squire in which he claimed total innocence but I'm afraid that DNA evidence is pretty damaging."

"I know. I guess they found his fingerprints all over his stick. Did they find any others?"

"Not that I know of. The one troubling question is why is he claiming he lost the stick? Your mother volunteered he came to her house the day after the murder looking for it."

"I know, she told me. Jake, you must know he didn't do this!"

"I do find it hard to believe he would be capable of such a thing. But who else might be involved?"

Mib took a long sip from her Chardonnay and carefully placed her glass in front of her. "When I had my visit with Uncle Ash I asked him about his relationship with Angie and he said they shared a love of poetry. He also said she had written some poems about a man she was involved with. One that he guessed might be, as he put it, 'unavailable.'"

"Married you mean?"

"That's my guess. Have the police found out where she lived? Have they searched her place?"

"That's on the docket. She lived in that trailer park off of Route 80."

"Tell them to look for some kind of journal or diary. It might have some clues as to this mystery man's identity."

"Good thought. I'll call them in the morning. What's that delicious smell?"

"I hope you like an old-fashioned stew. Bring your beer and we'll have dinner in the dining room."

I made a point of never sitting near her tables
when I came to the coffee shop but I noticed
the two of you were always cozy. And then I
noticed you had left your walking stick in the
hat rack that day so I slipped it under my coat
and left the two of you gabbing away.

CHAPTER **SEVEN**

WHEN GRACE DOUBLEDAY MARRIED Josh
Reynolds, Archie Crawford, the self-appointed
town historian, declared the match "a uniting of
dynasties." Grace had thought it foolish at the time
but, after all, Abner Doubleday and Josiah Reynolds
were part of that hardy band who followed Henry
Whitfield across the ocean to settle on the shores of
Long Island Sound in 1639.

Josiah was a blacksmith who soon opened a
forge and began plying his trade, which grew into
the Reynolds Foundry, which provided a handsome
income for the family until the early seventies when
Josh, who was then the president, closed its doors

and sold off the property for a good profit. Abner was a farmer who plowed the rich acres to the north of town. The Doubleday farms are currently run by a group of his descendants. There wasn't a time when Grace drove past the Whitfield House that she didn't think of her ancestor cooped up inside. "No wonder Henry Whitfield went back to England!"

For some reason, Grace was remembering her wedding this particular morning. *I've got to get Phil Edwards over here to move the washer and dryer up to the first floor. These stairs will be the death of me* she thought as she pushed the laundry basket up the stairs ahead of her. When she reached the kitchen she pushed the basket under the table and poured herself a second cup of coffee.

She had been thinking about his wedding as she sorted Squire's laundry. *He looked so handsome on his wedding day. He was always particular about his clothes.* Grace and Josh and Ash had grown up together. And, when they reached high school, Grace and Josh became a couple. Josh loved sports and played tackle on the football team. Ash chose fencing and began wearing a cape which led to his nickname. He played the lead in the senior play and that's when he fell in love with Lucy Steward, who played opposite him.

They were such a wonderful couple and Ash adored little Annabelle. The guilt he felt after the accident almost killed him. It really is a miracle he's able to function as well as he does. I think his writing has saved him. She poured the remains of her cup in the sink and reached for the thermos. She had been driving into New Haven every day to bring her brother-in-law his laundry and mail.

I wish Carl had been able to persuade him to hire a decent lawyer. I know he's innocent but I'm afraid a young public defender isn't really up to the job of defending him properly. Grace was puzzled by her son's apparent lack of interest in the case although she knew he was totally absorbed in his First Selectman victory. Mib had been a great help and Grace was delighted she was dating Jake Donaldson. Mib and Carl had never been close and Carl's treatment of his younger sister always bothered their mother. She loved her son, but sometimes she didn't like him very much. Josh, on the other hand, worshiped his football star son and turned a blind eye to any faults he might have.

She filled a Tupperware container with some cinnamon rolls hoping to bribe the nice guard to perhaps share them with Squire. She tightened the lid on the thermos, grabbed her keys and reached for the laundry bag. *Please, God, help us all, especially Ash.*

CHAPTER **EIGHT**

"HEY, FRANK...take a look at this..."

The two CSI technicians were combing through Angie Loomis' trailer searching for evidence. One of them had picked up a quilted pink notebook.

"Hey, hey...what have we here? Pretty hot stuff!"

"What's that? Her diary?"

"Sort of. More like some poems about her boyfriend."

"Is this the guy they have in custody?"

"Well, if it is, I have to admire him. He's in his seventies and this gal was 23. Hard to believe he could satisfy her, if you know what I mean."

"Let's check his medicine cabinet for Viagra when we search his place."

They didn't find much of anything in Squire's room, I guess it was pretty monastic." Jake and Mib were having dinner at Guilford Mooring and he was filling her in with the latest details on the case. "They did find something of interest in Angie's trailer, however."

"Some of her poems perhaps?"

"Yep. Apparently there were some pretty hot poems about her boyfriend. The techies wondered if Squire was taking Viagra but they didn't find anything when they searched"

When Mib got home that night she gave her brother a call. "Hi Carl, hope I'm not calling too late."

"No, no. Betsy and I just got back from Greg's basketball game. He's doing real well, shot five baskets. Guess he's following in the footsteps of your boyfriend, the Chief."

"He's not my boyfriend, thank you. The reason I'm calling is to ask you if you knew Angie Loomis."

"Who me? Why would I know her? Oh, I guess I knew she was a waitress at the coffee shop but, other than that, no. Why do you ask?"

"She apparently had a lover, probably a married man, and I just wondered if you had heard any talk about it."

"News to me. But, like I said, I didn't know her or anything about her."

"Sorry I bothered you. I'm just so worried about Uncle Ash and am searching for anything that might help save him from a conviction."

"No bother at all. How's the old boy doing? I have been so tied up at Town Hall I haven't had a chance to get into New Haven to see him. I'll do that first thing next week."

From the time they were children Mib always knew when her brother was lying. Like the time the cows were "tipped" at the Doubleday farm. Of course Carl claimed to be totally innocent and their father bought it, as always. Mib and her mother knew better. There was something in his voice that let Mib know he was probably the ringleader.

Like tonight on the phone when she asked about Angie Loomis.

MY MAN

You say that you're too old for me,

But I'm afraid I disagree,

In my arms where you belong,

You are hot and hard and strong.

----

*Shit. When they did the autopsy
I hope they didn't find out about the
baby. And, if they do, I sure as hell
hope they don't take any DNA samples.*

CHAPTER NINE

"HI JAKE, hope I'm not calling at a bad time."

"No, no, as a matter of fact, I was just thinking about you. What's up?"

"Are they going to do an autopsy on Angie Loomis?"

"Already have...why?"

"Will they check to see if she was pregnant?"

"Do you think she might have been?"

"Just a hunch...and, if they do find that out, would they examine the fetus and check its DNA?"

"I don't know but I can find out. Why don't you meet me at Quattro's for a drink. Say, around 5:30?"

"See you then, and thanks."

Mib often thought that hiring her sister in law to work at the shop was the best decision she ever made. Betsy knew everyone in town and loved clothes. Her enthusiasm and charm were contagious, making MIB the talk of Guilford. And today was no exception. The shop was filled with shoppers when Cheryl Henderson walked in. The yacht club dance was coming up and Fred had insisted she get something new to wear.

"Cheryl, how nice to see you. Looking for something for the dance?" Betsy gave her a warm hug and led her to a rack of cocktail dresses. "You're a size 8 aren't you? I think this cobalt blue dress would be great on you."

"I like it and I like the red one too. Are you and Carl coming to the dance?"

"Yes, why don't you sit at our table?"

"We'd love to join you. Have you had any news about Carl's uncle?"

"My mother-in-law goes to New Haven every day and I worry about her. His trial is coming up next week and things don't look good."

"I feel so bad about all of this. Squire has always been so gracious, I can't believe he would be capable of such a thing. In fact, I think I may know something that might help him."

"Oh?"

CHAPTER **TEN**

WHEN HE GRADUATED from Yale Law School that spring, unlike his fellow graduates who joined white- shoe law firms in New York, Jason Bernstein was delighted to land a spot at the Public Defender's office in New Haven. But this latest case had him buffaloed. He knew his client was innocent but how to prove it?

"Mr. Reynolds, I strongly feel someone has framed you. Do you have any enemies?"

"Oh, good heavens, no! I know I'm regarded as something of an oddity in our town, but I can't imagine anyone wishing me harm."

In preparing for the trial, which was on the docket for the following week, Jason had lined up quite a group of character witnesses. Fearing the prosecutor would use his client's mental frailty against him, he had contacted the therapist who had treated Squire when he was at Gladewood. "I can't violate doctor-patient privilege, as you know, but I am happy to testify that it is my firm belief Ashley Reynolds is totally incapable of committing such a vicious and violent act."

Jason leafed through the file from his briefcase. "The crime lab uncovered a book of poetry in the victim's trailer. Do you have any idea who her lover might be?"

"I can tell you it certainly wasn't me! But I gathered from the poems she shared with me that he was somewhat older than she and possibly married. Is that of any benefit to my case?"

"Perhaps we should interview her fellow employees at the coffee shop. Maybe they know who it might be. Possibly a customer?"

"She was such a pretty little thing. I'm sure she had a ton of admirers so it couldn't hurt to ask."

"An autopsy has been performed and there was no evidence of a pregnancy, which was a thought of mine as a possible motive for her murder. So that leaves us up the creek as far as the identity of her lover. The one question in this whole thing is the fact that your walking stick went missing before the crime was committed. Do you remember the last time you saw it?"

"Strangely enough...I think it was at the Coffee Shop. I always left it leaning up against the coat rack and, when I came to get it, it was gone. Several people will tell you I was searching high and low for it."

"Yes, but we have to prove you were missing it prior to the murder, and how do we do that?"

No baby? How did I get so lucky?
They'll never find me now!

CHAPTER **ELEVEN**

MIB WAS IN HER OFFICE at the back of the shop when she overheard Betsy in conversation with a customer.

"Did Carl have a chance to get in touch with that lawyer?" Cheryl asked.

"He promised to call him. I assumed they would be in touch with you by now. I'll check with Carl and see if he's heard anything."

"Ask Carl about what?" Mib poked her head out of her office. "Sorry to be so nosy but I couldn't help but overhear."

"Oh, that was Cheryl Henderson. We had to special order that red cocktail dress in her size. She told me something interesting the last time she was here."

"Interesting how?"

"Apparently she ran into Squire the night before the murder and noticed he didn't have his walking stick with him."

"And you told Carl about this?"

"I sure did. He said he would get in touch with the guy who's representing Squire but Cheryl has heard nothing so I'd better double check."

"Public Defender's Office."

"May I speak to Jason Bernstein?"

"Who's calling?"

"This is Mary Beth Reynolds."

Betsy, can you come in here for a minute?" Since the shop was empty, Betsy was able to join Mib in her office. "What's up?"

"I spoke with the young lawyer who's representing Uncle Ash and he said he hadn't heard from Carl, even though he was in to see Squire last week."

"That's odd. I wonder if he said anything about it to Squire?"

"Apparently not. Betsy, I don't want to put you on the spot, but I have reason to believe Carl may know more about this case than he's letting on. Do you have access to his computer?"

"Yes, I do."

"How about his iPhone?"

"That too."

"Would you be willing to do a little sleuthing to see if he has any interesting messages on either one of them?"

"Interesting how?"

"I don't know how else to put this. I think it's possible Carl knew Angie Loomis and may have been involved with her."

"Involved in what way?"

"I don't want to upset you, but I think they may have been lovers."

Betsy returned home that evening and walked into her empty kitchen with a heavy heart. Once again Carl was out for the evening, this time attending a Zoning Board of Appeals meeting... or was he? The past six years of their marriage had been filled with these empty nights but when Mib brought up the idea of an affair, she had dismissed it out of hand.

It's only natural for married couples to cool down in the romance department, isn't it? After all, we've been together for over 30 years now. She put the kettle on for a cup of tea and sat at the kitchen table remembering. *He has been particularly distant this past year but I thought it was because of the campaign. Maybe I should take a look at his computer...or, maybe not. We have too much to lose if he's involved in this. But, on the other hand, I hate to see Squire be the sacrificial lamb. I have never believed he was guilty but who else could have done this? Was Carl sleeping with that little tramp from the coffee shop?*

When Carl got home from the meeting around 10 that night he found Betsy asleep at the table, an empty tea cup beside her. "Honey? Are you okay?" He shook her shoulder gently, startled to see an almost fearful look on her face when she came to.

"I'm fine. Busy day at the shop, I guess. Did you have some dinner?"

"Yeah, I ended up at Guilford Mooring with Bud Henry after the zoning meeting. He bought me dinner. I hope he wasn't trying to bribe me, he's applied for a variance on that property on River Street and has some stiff opposition from the neighbors. You ready to pack it in?"

"Carl, sit down for a minute. Did you know that girl at the coffee shop?"

"What? You mean the one who was murdered? What is all this? Mib was asking me about that too!"

"That's why I'm asking. Mib wanted me to check your computer and iPhone for information. She thinks you might have had an affair with that girl."

"Oh my God. I know my sister and I aren't exactly bosom buddies, but this is ridiculous!"

"I know, I know. I'm sorry I brought it up. I'll tell her to drop it. It's really my fault that all this came up in the first place. I was talking with Cheryl Henderson at the shop and Mib overheard us. But I am glad that Cheryl has decided to testify about seeing Squire that night. I thought I told you."

"What night? What are you talking about?"

"Cheryl ran into him in the parking lot of Cox School the night before the murder and he didn't have his walking stick with him. She thought it was odd that he would be walking in the dark without it and is willing to testify."

"Good. Look, honey, I know I haven't been the most attentive husband lately but I've been so tied up with the election and all the town hall stuff. Listen, let's have dinner at Chapter One tomorrow night, just you and me. How about it?"

CHAPTER TWELVE

WHEN BETSY CAME TO WORK the next morning she went straight to Mib's office. "I talked to Carl last night and he got pretty upset when I asked about the girl. He says you asked about her too. I guess he thinks this is kind of a witch hunt."

"Did you ask him why he didn't tell Squire's lawyer about Cheryl and the walking stick?"

"I guess I forgot to tell him. He was so mad at me for asking about the girl that I got flustered."

"Betsy, I'm sorry I got you involved in this. Let's let it go, okay?"

When Cheryl went to her mailbox two mornings later she found a message that someone had pasted together with mismatched letters: You Have a Nice Family. Stay away from the courtroom.

Well, I'll be darned. This definitely proves Squire isn't the killer. She marched into her kitchen and picked up the phone. "Hi, Mib, this is Cheryl Henderson. I am more determined than ever to speak in court but I think I'm going to need a police escort. I just got a threatening note in my mailbox."

Hi Jake. I just got off the phone with Cheryl Henderson. She found a note in her mailbox this morning warning her not to go to court, which I think definitely proves Squire isn't the killer."

"Wow. This is getting hinkier by the minute. Looks like she needs some protection here."

"She is determined to testify but she thinks she needs a police escort."

"When's she slated to appear?"

"Friday at ten."

"That eliminates me...I'm speaking at Guilford Lakes that morning about drug prevention. Look, let me see who's available and I'll assign someone to drive her to New Haven."

---

*Stupid busybody. I guess she decided
not to pay attention to my note.
She's going to regret that.*

CHAPTER **THIRTEEN**

"I'M WORRIED ABOUT CHERYL." Mib reached across Jake's chest for the packet of matches on the other side of the bed. "Mom would kill me if she knew I smoked, but I'm just so upset about this business with Cheryl."

"I don't like your smoking either, honey, but if it's giving you some kind of relief, I guess I have to go along with it." Jake took the matchbook and lit her cigarette. He was spending a lot of time at her apartment, almost living there. Mib had suggested he move in, but he knew the talk that would cause in the town. He leaned back against the headboard and turned to her. "Look, everything is going to be fine. I wish I could drive her but I've got to give one of those 'Say No to Drugs' talks at the school on that day. I've asked Chuck to step in for me and all will be fine."

"I just can't believe Carl would write that note."

"I can't believe it either. I don't know why you're so dead set on the idea that he's the killer."

"Well, I was "dead set" until the business of the note. I can easily believe he was fooling around with that girl, but to be stupid enough to threaten Cheryl about testifying? That just proves our uncle is innocent!"

"What gets me is how many people knew about Cheryl's testimony? Me, you, Betsy, and I guess Betsy must have told Carl. Did Fred Henderson know about it?"

"Yes, and Cheryl said he didn't want her to testify. The only other people who knew were Uncle Ash and his attorney, Jason Bernstein. Does the prosecution know what her testimony is about?"

"I doubt it. They probably have seen her name on the witness list and think she's yet another character reference for Squire."

"What about your staff at the station? Who knew about it? Anybody?"

"I had to tell Chuck, of course, but I don't think anybody else knows about it." He took the last of her cigarette from her fingers and stubbed it out in the ashtray on the bedside table. "Listen, I've got a much better idea of relieving your stress," turning off the lamp and taking her into his arms.

CHAPTER **FOURTEEN**

"HONEST TO GOD, CHIEF. It was the damnedest thing." Chuck Hopwood sat at Jake's desk in a state of disbelief. "I decided to take the scenic route into New Haven, you know, along Route 146? I thought it might be calming for her. She seemed to be a little on edge."

"Well, that's understandable. Go on." Jake looked up from his notepad, wishing a lawyer was in the room.

"We got to the top of the hill, you know, past the causeway, and...all of a sudden...this guy wearing a ski mask jumps out from behind the rocks right in front of the car. I swerved and slammed on the brakes and, the next thing I knew, he ran to the side of the car, opened the door and grabbed her. I had her in the front seat, did I tell you that?"

"No...you forgot to mention that. You should have known better, Chuck."

"I know, I know...but I was worried about her, uh, condition, ya know? Anyways, I shut down the car and ran around to her side but by then he had hit her and run off. I didn't know whether to run after him or look after her and, at that point, another car came up the hill and you know the rest."

"What did he hit her with? Could you tell?"

"Whatever it was, he ran off with it."

"It's a damned good thing that other car came along or Cheryl would be dead, instead of being in the ICU at St. Raph's." Jake put his pen down and leaned back in his chair. "I have to agree with you, Chuck. This is pretty unbelievable."

Fred Henderson sat slumped in a chair in the waiting room outside the ICU waiting for an update on his wife's condition. He felt the hum of his cell phone and answered the call. "Oh, hi Mom. How are the girls? Good, good. Thanks so much for taking them to school. Will you be able to pick them up at 3:15? I don't know when I'll get out of here. No...no word from the doctor as yet. I'll let you know as soon as I hear anything and bless you for all your help." *Why did I let her do it? Why? I begged her not to get involved but she wouldn't listen. Please God... please don't let her die. Please...*

"Mr. Henderson? Excuse me, I'm Mark Larsen, the neurologist assigned to your wife's case?"

"Oh, yes, Doctor. Sorry I didn't hear you coming. Too busy praying, I guess. What's the latest on Cheryl?"

"The good news is she will recover. She's conscious and conversant. The not-so-good news is she seems to have a loss of memory, maybe due to the trauma of the event and one that will lift after time. We really can't say at this point."

"You mean she isn't able to remember the attack?"

"Not at this time."

"Will she know me?"

"I'm sure she will...why don't you go in and find out."

CHAPTER **FIFTEEN**

MELANIE HOPWOOD prided herself on her housekeeping. The small split-level house she shared with her husband was immaculate, especially now that their kids were up and grown. The one exception was Chuck's "Man Cave," a small room in the basement which he kept literally under lock and key, preventing any invasion of vacuum cleaner or dust cloth.

On this particular morning, when Melanie pulled into the garage, she happened to glance over at the padlocked door and noticed a bag of trash in front of it. "Now that's great...he couldn't even dump his trash in the recycling bin?" She marched over

in a huff and picked up the black bag, surprised
at its weight. "What's he got in here? Gold bars?"
Intrigued, she untied the handles to take a look at
the contents. "Magazines? Is this what he does down
here...read magazines?" And then she glimpsed a
copy of *Oprah Magazine* she had been looking for
in search of a recipe for rhubarb custard pie. "I've
been searching high and low for this. What on earth
would Chuck want with a copy of *Oprah*?" In rifling
through the magazine, she discovered many pages
had been torn out of it. Why? "Well Mr. Charles
Henry Hopwood, you and I are going to have a little
chat when you get home."

CHAPTER **SIXTEEN**

"LADIES AND GENTLEMEN OF THE JURY,"
Jason approached the jury box with a document in
his hand. "The Court has graciously allowed me to
present evidence to you, due to the absence of our
witness, Mrs. Cheryl Henderson, who is unable to be
with us today due to the fact that she is a patient in
the Intensive Care Unit at St. Raphael's Hospital."

After the judge pounded his gavel to quiet the
gasps and chatter that filled the courtroom, Jason
was able to continue. "I am not allowed to share
with you the testimony Mrs. Henderson would have
given. However, I am allowed to present evidence,
entered into the docket as Exhibit A, which shows

that her testimony was very threatening to a certain individual."

Jason paused and then handed a piece of paper to the foreman of the jury. "This is what Cheryl Henderson found in her mailbox five days before she was scheduled to appear before you." He carefully observed the faces of the jurors as they passed the paper between themselves and was pleased to note the unvarying expression of distaste on their faces.

"It gets worse. As she was being driven to the court by a Guilford police officer, a man wearing a ski mask jumped in front of car, causing the officer to swerve to the side of the road and stop the car. By the time the officer was able to get out of the car, the man opened the passenger side door, grabbed Mrs. Henderson and beat her on the back of her head." The courtroom once again had to be silenced by the judge's pounding gavel. "Fortunately, another car approached before the man could beat her any further and he ran off into the woods. I'm happy to report that Cheryl Henderson has survived the attack and is recovering well, although she currently has no memory of the terrible incident. Her attacker remains at large."

The foreman of the jury reached forward and handed the paper back to the young attorney. "Thank you, Mr. Foreman. Ladies and gentlemen, I think each of the incidents clearly proves that my client is not guilty of the crime for which he has been charged and I ask, in light of this evidence, that you will find him innocent of the charge."

CHAPTER **SEVENTEEN**

GRACE STOOD IN THE DINGY waiting room outside the cellblock of the New Haven Courthouse waiting for her brother-in-law. She had brought fresh clothes and delighted to see him walking down the narrow hallway, his cape draped around him and his hat at a jaunty angle.

"Hope I get my walking stick back," he said as he gave her a hug, "I feel kind of naked without it!"

"You look great, Ash. Let's get out of here."

"I have to meet with Jason at his office before we head back home. I owe him so much."

"Is he far from here?"

"No, no, just a block up Whitney Avenue. Do you want to come with me? Or would you rather wait?"

"I'll come with you. We all owe that young man a big thank you."

"No one more than I. We were blessed when the judge allowed him to present the letter. I had a bad moment when the prosecutor claimed I could have hired someone to do all this dirty work but I could tell the members of the jury clearly weren't investing in that theory. And young Mr. Bernstein did himself proud in his summing up. Yes, I am a very lucky man. But who is this killer? He must be found before any further damage can be done!"

By the time they got back to her house, the twosome were, as Squire put it, "rather weary." "Are you hungry? Why don't I scramble up some eggs and I can toast that cinnamon raisin bread you like so much."

"That sounds heavenly, Grace. But shouldn't I be getting back to my own room?"

Grace took down the omelet pan and opened the refrigerator door for the eggs and butter. "I'm sorry to tell you this, but your room is no longer available. I had your things moved to Carl's old room on the third floor. And that's where you are going stay from now on...no ifs ands or buts!"

"Oh, Grace, I couldn't invade your privacy!"

"Invade my privacy, my foot! If I'm going to stay in this old rattletrap I'm going to need some support and you're just the man for the job." She poured the beaten eggs into the sizzling butter and turned to fill the kettle with water for tea.

CHAPTER **EIGHTEEN**

"OKAY, SO MY UNCLE DIDN'T DO IT. Who did?"

Mib sat across from Jake on her living room sofa, longing for a cigarette. Her lover shifted in his chair uncomfortably, wishing he could give her a ready answer.

"Look, Jake, we always knew Squire wasn't the killer. But who on earth had so much knowledge about the case? We eliminated Carl after the note and especially after the attack on Cheryl. But could he have hired someone to do this?"

"If he did, it would have to be somebody directly involved...somebody on my staff I guess. No, no I don't think Carl is involved. I'm beginning to think it has to be Chuck."

"Chuck Hopwood? Oh my God…that fits, doesn't it? I have been wondering about his story about the guy in the ski mask. How could he have known the direction Chuck took?"

Hi Melanie, this is Jake Donaldson. Is Chuck at home?"

"Oh, hi, Chief. No…he left earlier this morning. I'm sorry to say we had a big fight and he took off."

"A fight about what?"

"Oh, he got mad at me because I nagged at him about a bag of trash."

"What about it?"

"Well, he has this 'Man Cave' in the basement that I'm not allowed to come near and the other day I found a bag of trash in front of it. It was filled with cutup magazines, if you can believe that. Anyway, when I went after him about it he got furious and accused me of snooping. I tried to reason with him but he ran down to the basement and took off in his truck like a bat outta hell!"

"Is the bag still there?"

"No, I looked. I guess he took it with him?"

S tate Police Headquarters, how can I direct your call?"

"This is Chief Donaldson in Guilford. I need an immediate APB for a 2002 Gray Datsun Pickup, CT license number GSO 324. The suspect may be armed and is a safety risk."

---

*How could I have been fucking
stupid? No way out here. So long,
Mel, sorry it had to end this way.*

CHAPTER **NINETEEN**

CHARLIE AND RALPH sat at their usual booth at the back of the coffee shop deep in conversation about the latest development in "The Case," as they chose to call it.

"I just can't get over it. Remember Chuck sat right here and said he couldn't say anything because he might lose his job!"

"I remember. It's just a damned shame he had to kill himself. I know he must have wanted to avoid a trial and prison, but when they found him he had the bag of cut up magazines and his gun which had traces of Cheryl Henderson's DNA on it, his goose was cooked."

"Huh. I guess he used his weapon to hit her on the back of the head. That was pretty dumb. And, since he was a suicide, his wife won't get any life insurance. That is, if there was any. Plus, no pension. Dumb all around. Not to mention getting caught up with Angie in the first place!"

"Yeah, it's a shame alright…hey, look who just walked in!"

Squire doffed his hat at Doreen, the cashier, then hung it on a peg and plunked his walking stick on the rack beneath it. "Your usual table, Squire?"

"Yes, thank you, Doreen. But first I need a word with Charlie Mayfield, if you don't mind." He headed for the back of the room, greeting many smiling faces on his way.

"Hey, Squire! Good to have you back."

"Thank you, Charlie, it's good to see you. And you too, Ralph."

"Won't you join us?"

"No, no, I don't want to intrude. I just wanted to ask how the booklet is coming along?"

"Oh, I was going to call you when I got back to the shop. All done. And I think you'll be pleased with it."

"I know I will and many thanks to you for continuing with it under such difficult circumstances."

"Oh, gosh, Squire, we always knew you couldn't have done it!"

"Bless you for your faith in me. I'll drop by later to pick up the books. I know Grace is looking forward to seeing it. Now excuse me while I get back to my table. I'm so happy to be remembered here."

"Oh, Squire, how could we ever forget you?"

CHAPTER **TWENTY**

IT LOOKED LIKE EVERY LIGHT was on in the big house on Dunk Rock Road. Grace was hosting a double celebration on this early spring evening and the lilac bushes around her front porch were about to bloom.

One of the guests of honor was already seated at the head of the dining room table. Squire had hidden under his chair copies of the poetry book about to be sold by the Ladies Auxiliary. Each one with a special handwritten message for his fellow guests.

"We were about to give up on you," boomed Carl as Mib and Jake, the other two honored guests, made their way to the table.

"Sorry about to be late, Mrs. Reynolds. There was a nasty pile up on 95, which is why I was late in picking up my fiancée."

"That's Grace to you, Jake. Please have a seat. I believe Ash was about to propose a toast."

All eyes turned to the head of the table as Squire rose, glass in hand. "First I want to honor my brother. I know how proud he would be of his son, our third-term First Selectman, and of his daughter, not only a successful business owner but soon to be wed to our valiant Chief of Police. All of them were so helpful in vindicating my name." He took a celebratory sip of his wine and began to carve the leg of lamb.

With that, Jake rose, raised his glass and said, "Not only am I blessed to be marrying a wonderful woman, I am honored to become a member of such an illustrious family."

He was followed by Carl, who stood, glass in hand. "So my baby sister finally landed herself a husband. Congrats Mib, welcome Jake, and three cheers for Squire!"

Mib held her tongue. Some things never change. Once a jerk, always a jerk. "I would like to make a final toast to my dear mother. She has been the heart of my family forever. Long may she wave!"

Grace bowed her head and prayed, "Thank you for the world so sweet. Thank you for the food we eat. Thank you for the birds that sing. Thank you, God, for everything."

"Now, Betsy, please pass the mashed potatoes."

J uliana Harris has contributed poems to *The New York Times*, *The Mid-America Poetry Review*, *The Best Times*, *Chicken Soup for the Soul* and *The Kansas City Star*, among other publications. A native of Kansas City, Missouri, she now lives in Guilford, CT where she is a member of the Guilford Poets Guild.

CPSIA information can be obtained
at www.ICGtesting.com
Printed in the USA
LVHW070350140621
690153LV00029B/986